Twelve ^More Little Race Cars

To our little race fans
Lauren and Taylor and Cameron

ISBN 0-9670600-1-X

Twelve More Little Race Cars / by Scott and Judy Pruett
Design and Art Direction: Glen Eytchison
Character Design and Illustration Rick Morgan

Special thanks to our "art guy" Glen Eytchison, for his talent, patience,
humor, and friendship.

Twelve More Little Race Cars

by

Scott and Judy Pruett

Design and Art Direction by Glen Eytchison
Illustrations by Rick Morgan

Word Weaver Books, Inc., Zephyr Hts., Nevada

Twelve race car drivers putting on their suits,
fireproof underwear and fireproof boots.

Starting up their engines, but one won't go,
one little race car doesn't make the show.

Eleven little race cars coming fast to race,
all drivers trying to set the pace.

One bumps another. Hey! That was mean,
one little race car won't take the green.

Ten little race cars zooming 'round the track,
one flips over and lands on its back.

The announcer yells, "OH NO, NOT THAT!"
One little race car cleared off the track.

Nine little race cars all running lean,
the race is both of man and machine.

Eight little race cars to the pits for fuel,
the crews are ready, and they look really cool.

The driver pulls up and hits his mark,
the engine stalls and won't re-start!

Seven little race cars running three abreast,
one spins out and now it's a mess.

The safety crew takes the driver away,
he's out of the race, but he's okay.

Six little race cars jockey for the lead,
they zip through the turns at a high rate of speed.

All of a sudden, just a wink of an eye,
the lead car stops and the rest go by.

He slides down the track, headed for
for the wall. This little car won't finish at all.

Four little race cars getting close to the end,
moving really fast as they're coming 'round the bend.

One loses his gears and he starts to slow,
poor little race car, that's no way to go!

Three little race cars drafting down the back,
one hits debris and his tire is going flat.

He went to the pit, the crew knew what to do,
but the tire rolled away and then there were two.

Two little race cars down to the wire,
one overheats and catches on fire.

The corner workers rush with some water to spray. One little car is done for the day.

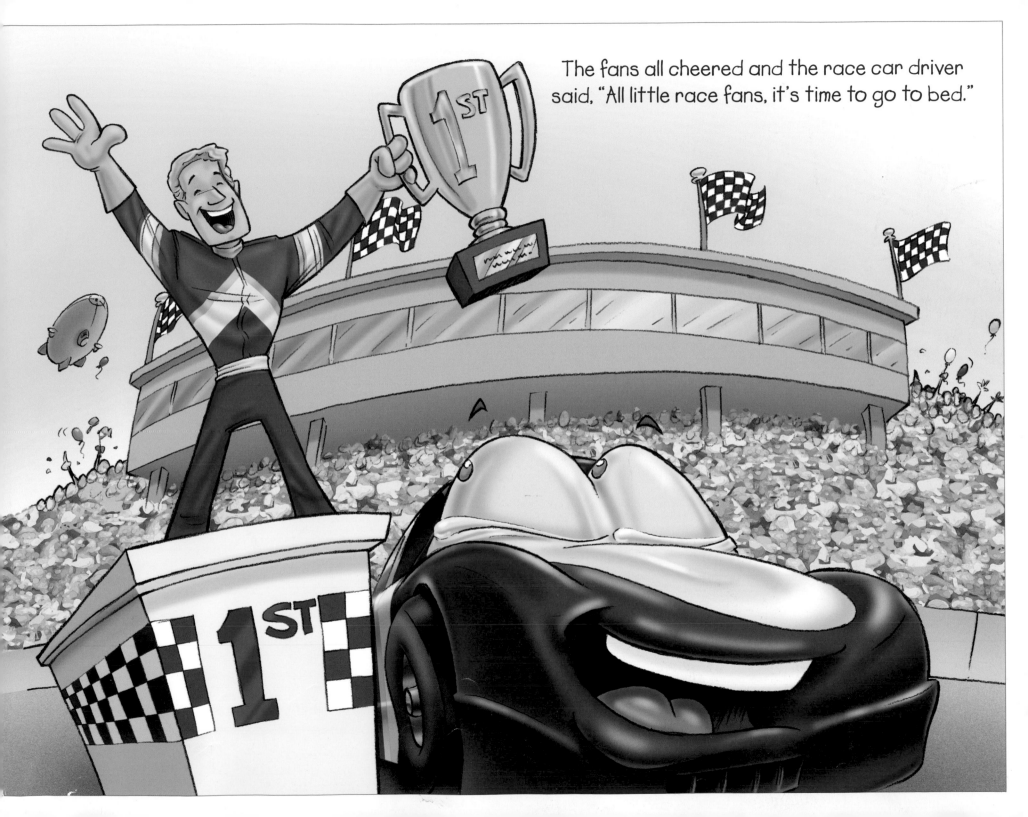

The fans all cheered and the race car driver said, "All little race fans, it's time to go to bed."

Would you like to order another book for yourself as a keepsake or a gift for a friend?

Simply copy and complete the form below. Mail it along with your payment to:
Word Weaver Books, Inc., 5951 Sandy Road, Loomis, California 95650
Check or money order only; please print clearly; allow 6-8 weeks for delivery.

Name: _____   Phone: _____

Address: _____

City: _____   State: _____ Zip: _____

Price: $12.95 per book

Shipping:
(1-2 Books $5.00)
(3-4 Books $10.00)
Orders outside the U.S. $18.00
per book plus shipping.

Sales Tax: If ordering from within
the state of Nevada, please add
7% of total

Quantity Ordered _____ Subtotal _____

Sales Tax .... _____

Shipping .... _____

Total .... _____

Visit us at our web site: **www.wordweaverbooks.com** for more **Twelve Little Race Cars** collectables.

Word Weaver

About the Authors

Scott and Judy Pruett live with their children Lauren, Taylor and Cameron, in McMinnville, Oregon.

Scott, a professional race car driver, began his career racing Go-Karts at the age of eight. Through hard work and determination he worked his way up the "racing ladder" winning numerous professional and non-professional titles, including: 1986 and 1988 IMSA Champion; 1987 and 1994 Trans Am Champion; and 1989 Indy 500 Rookie of the Year. He raced ten years in the C.A.R.T. series, Championship Auto Racing Teams (formerly known as Indy Cars), achieving three victories, seven poles, numerous podium finishes and was very instumental in Firestones return to, and success in, racing. In 2000, Scott completed his first full season in the Nascar Winston Cup Series driving the #32 Tide taurus. Scott competed in the Trans-Am Series in 2003, capturing his third championship. He is currently competing in the Grand American Rolex Series, as well as selected Nascar races for Ganassi Racing.

Judy is an Occupational Therapist with fifteen years of experience ranging from Child Development to Sports Medicine. She currently enjoys raising their three children, training with Scott, exploring the outdoors, music, theatre and writing.

In 1999, Scott and Judy formed Word Weaver Books to bring their love of racing to the world of children's publishing.

Autographs